For more information, address:
theworldkeepersbooks@gmail.com

FIRST EDITION

www.tythehunter.com

For Jenny, my favorite sounding board!

ABOUT THE AUTHOR

Check Ty The Hunter's website to
see a complete list of books.

The World Keepers -
Tween/Teen readers

The Guild Crafters -
Tween/Teen Readers

The Guild Crafters Block Books
- New Readers

While you're there, don't forget to ask your parents
to download your free book.

If you'd like to see Ty play Rescue Mission Zombie
Assault for the first time, *click here*.
Don't forget to SUBSCRIBE!

You can also find the videos on
www.TyTheHunter.com under VIDEOS

Get in touch with me at
theworldkeepersbooks@gmail.com

CHAPTER 1

JED WANTS ANSWERS OR DOES HE?

Three Days.

72 Hours.

Four Thousand Three Hundred Twenty Minutes.

That's how long it's been since I woke up in Thomas's room after escaping Roblox.

Such a long time, but not enough time.

A long time because I haven't heard from anyone yet, and I do want answers. Not enough time because I'm scared of what will happen once I do have answers.

Sometimes, ignorance is bliss.

Like now, maybe?

Still, you'd think I'd have some of it figured out. You'd think I'd have done some research, made some connections in my brain, come up with my own answers.

I haven't, but it's not for lack of trying, you're going to have to take my word for that.

Do you know what happens when you google "I got trapped in a video game"? Well, seeing as how I'm a professional with those search terms right now, I'll share with you.

Nothing helpful happens.

You get a bunch of ads for....

Wait for it.

....

.....

Video games.

You also get ads for books about video games, movies about video games, and even forums where people are sure this has happened to them.

I did find out that people who claim to have been sucked into video games have an extremely high rate of alien abduction.

Also, thanks to these searches, I'm probably on a watch list for those folks in the United States who might pose a threat to national security.

You'd think I'd have talked to Thomas, too, right? You're like "Well Jed, why didn't you call your brother as soon as you came back?"

One step ahead of you, my friend. I TRIED to call Thomas.

Turns out, he didn't bring his phone because he knew he wouldn't have any service.

The lease is out in the middle of nowhere, Texas (also known as Post, go google it).

It has a population of 5,186 or something like that, half of those are probably cows.

You see a lot of tumbleweeds, a lot of deer, a lot of quail, and more than your fair share of trucks. There is also a very high ratio of people to small 4 wheel drive vehicles.

What you don't see is a lot of bars on your cell phone screen.

So, here I am, three days later, knowing not a single thing more than I knew when Ty dragged me back into my world.

There you go! You are now in the know! Well, as much in the know as I can possibly make you.

I know you want answers, heck, I want answers. I hate to burst your bubble, dear reader, but I have none. My answer pockets are empty....

My dad did bring his cell phone, I know that much, but he hasn't called yet. Even if he did call, I'm not sure he'd be on the phone long enough to put Thomas on.

I'm also not sure Thomas would have enough privacy to talk to me about the things I'd want to talk about.

He's only supposed to be gone for a week. I have to console myself with that. Just four more extremely long days, and then I'll have some answers, hopefully.

I'm thanking my lucky stars that dad didn't take Ty on this trip. He usually does, almost without fail. It just so happens that Ty was chasing a stick the other day, bolting over the grass with that "all or nothing" run he has, when he landed badly in a hole, and hurt his paw.

The vet says he'll be fine, but he needs to rest it for a bit. If he goes hunting, he won't rest, he's not that kind of dog. So, no hunting for him.

Can you even imagine what would have happened had he not been home with me? What if he hadn't been in Thomas's room, sleeping on his bed, waking up when the portal appeared?

I can't think about it too hard, or it starts to make my stomach feel sick. I don't know if I'd have gotten through that portal without him. There was nothing else within easy reach. Nothing else I could have grabbed hold of to keep myself anchored.

Even if there had been, what good would it have done me? My ankle was so busted up that I couldn't even walk anymore.

There was no way I would have been able to fight ALL those guards trying to keep me from leaving.

So, I'm glad Ty's home, and he seems delighted to be here, my little partner in crime.

Well, not crime, but you know what I mean.

We've been hanging out constantly, he's loving the extra pets and treats. I even managed to sneak him some bacon from my breakfast this morning. I just slid it off my plate, into my lap, and Ty took it from there.

Mom's pretty strict about him not eating "people food". He may not be a people, but I know he likes bacon, and I love making him wag his tail.

Also, it's still freezing cold outside, so I'm more than happy to stick my feet under him while I sit on the couch. If I keep him happy, he's more likely to sit still while I do it.

It's a win/win situation for both of us. I feel safer with him around, though I really hope he never has to retrieve me from another dimension EVER again.

The cold snap is still snapping.

As I said, it's freezing! I would not be at all shocked if it snowed in the next couple of days!

The last time it snowed, Thomas was 2 and a half, and I was just a bump under mom's shirt, not even a very big bump!

You might think snow is no big deal (depending on where you're from), but we live in SOUTH TEXAS so it would be a big deal here.

Want to see the city of Houston shut down for a few days? Let a few white flakes fall from the sky. We will come to a complete standstill, I promise.

We don't have things like snow plows, salt for the roads, ice scrapers, or all-weather tires.

We have sun and heat, and a lot of rain during certain parts of the year. We also have loads of humidity, and mosquitoes that could LEGIT carry you away.

Typically, the cold weather wouldn't bother me at all. I'd just stay inside, read books, and play video games.

Maybe I'd go outside once in awhile to brave the cold and feel fantastic at how hardy and rugged I am.

I know, it makes me laugh when I say it, too.

Ever since the portal incident though, I haven't really felt like logging in.

I think it's understandable.

It took about a day and a half for me to want to get back on Roblox at all. When I did though, it was normal, like nothing ever happened. Little characters were running around everywhere. My "friend's list" was full of folks who messaged me asking if I wanted to do this thing or that thing with them.

It was all the same, like nothing had ever happened.

I know different, though. I know that game is not what it seems.

Kat promised she'd message me, but so far, I haven't heard from her. I also haven't heard from Jake, but he's not the one who said he'd be in touch, so I'm not expecting it.

I did look for both of them on the server, but no dice.

I thought about going through my friend's list and messaging everyone to ask if they were Kat or Jake. Then I thought, "how would you answer if you got a message saying, "Hey, is your real name Kat or Jake?

Did you help me escape the game a few days ago?""

I might even have done that if there was a name that had "Kat" or "Jake" in it, but there wasn't.

People don't use their real names in these games, mostly. If you look at my friend's list, it has names like:

Psychotron

Edrella

Flower

Madriel

Papanok

Pinkalishus

You don't see any people named "Mike" or "Mark" or "Jenny". Not that "Jenny" isn't a perfectly lovely name. It just doesn't sound very intimidating.

"Jenny has challenged you to a duel," doesn't evoke the same sense of dread as "Psychotron has challenged you to a duel."

Think about it, which one would you rather fight?

They could be the exact same person, but you'd be a little more scared of the guy with "Psycho" in his name, right?

So, no real names. I can't find them that way, or if they are using some part of their real name, they're not on my friend's list.

You see my dilemma....

I had also thought about getting on Thomas's computer and checking his friend's list, but I don't know his password.

I have a feeling that if anyone is friends with these people, it's him.

Checking his computer would be a great idea! If only I could do it. After all, they seemed to know him well, or at least know OF him.

I also thought about texting my dad, but what would I say? It all goes back to Thomas not having a place to talk to me in private, even if they did have service for a bit.

I thought too about just leaving it alone, pretending it never happened.

If I left it alone, I do wonder if he'd ever mention anything to me.

Would Kat see him in the game the next time he's on and tell him what went on? Or would she clam up about it? I'm convinced she's the reason I was in there at all.

What if whatever happened was meant for Thomas, instead of me?

That's what I think happened. I think I was the unwitting victim of "wrong place, wrong time."

After getting back home, I walked out of Thomas's room and went back to my room, hoping to catch a bit of sleep. I just needed two or three hours before mom woke me up for the day.

When I slept, it was fantastic, absolute bliss. I didn't dream about what happened, and when I woke up, I started to get on with my day like normal. It was a pretty great few minutes.

Then my ankle began to throb, and it all came back.

Part of me would love to think it was all a bad dream.

I'd like to believe that I really did something else to hurt myself, and my imagination just went wild.

Another part of me feels this urgency to find a way back into Roblox and figure out what's going on.

Even though I'm irritated at Kat, I haven't forgotten that she and Jake got caught, or at least one of them did.

What happened to them when they were caught? Are they okay? I keep thinking that I could be doing something to help.

Instead, I'm here, ignorant and feeling very incapable.

That's why I'm just sitting on the couch, enjoying the feel of the warm leather under my pajamas, watching TV and playing my iPad.

I wish I could ride my bike, I wish it were warm out, but I do not wish to be playing Roblox. It feels wrong now, after going through what I went through. You shouldn't fear for your life inside of a place that's supposed to be exciting and fun.

I've already asked myself if Kat and Jake were in there like I was. I still don't have a "for sure" answer, but I doubt it. I think they were watching me like I watch the other players on the screen.

What if those little-pixelated people are real?

I was there, I was real, so....

It doesn't bear thinking about.

CHAPTER 2

REDSTONE BLOCKS  NIK NAMES AND MOM IN FUZZY SOCKS

Let me tell you a more about the Redstone Block that started this whole ordeal.

I don't have any proof to back it up, but I do think that's how I ended up in Roblox.

I've thought about putting the batteries back in and turning it on. I'm not 100% sure the block had anything to do with it, and I'd like to test it.

But, what if it did, what if I'm right?

What if I turn it on and end up back in the game?

What if I don't have any help this time?

I won't be testing my theory.

Anyhow, my mom bought my brother this little grey block for Christmas 2 years ago.

He was going through a phase where he was scared of the dark. He was also completely into Minecraft. She said that when she saw this block, she thought it would help him get over his fear while also being "cool".

He still sleeps with a night-light, but don't tell him I told you.

The block is about 2 and a half inches square, and it's made of some sort of hard plastic. We've dropped it a billion times while we're playing. It's been stepped on, chucked at people, and hit by my head, but it keeps on working.

As long as it has fresh batteries, that thing is going to light up when you tap it.

It's supposed to look like a Minecraft Redstone Block. Just like in Minecraft, the grey is interspersed with bits of oddly shaped clear bits. They sort of remind me of clear Tetris pieces, you know?

When you tap the block, a light on the inside comes on and makes the clear pieces glow red. It has 3 levels of brightness. If you tap it once, it'll glow very softly. If you tap it again, the glow gets brighter. If you tape it a third time, it's enough to let you see your whole room, though not very well.

It doesn't have a timer, as far as I know, so it does go through a lot of batteries, especially if you leave it on too long. You have to tap it a fourth time to make it turn off, so think about it. If you're using it as a nightlight to help your fear of the dark, are you really going to turn it off to save batteries?

No?

Me neither.

I sort of broke the block when I came back through the portal.

Rather, it's not entirely broken, but enough that it's not going to turn on if I tap it.

The first thing I did after coming through was to grab it and hurl it against the wall. That was three days ago, I haven't messed with it since.

The battery panel snapped off, the batteries fell out, and how it landed is how it still sits on Thomas's floor.

No more glowing Redstone.

I'm not 100% sure that I got into the portal via that block, but it IS the last thing I touched before waking up in the game. I only touched it with the back of my head, but still. Given all the facts, I feel like it's a solid theory.

Like I said though, I don't want to test that theory.

This is why I was trying so hard to get in touch with Thomas, Kat, or Jake. Those guys know what's going on, and they know how to get in and out of the world without being trapped in it.

At least, I think they do.

There's so much I don't know.

All I know for sure is what Kat told me. "Get out before dark."

She said it was the most important thing, so I'm not going to forget it anytime soon.

The good thing about Thomas being gone for a week is that I can go in his room with impunity.

Mom doesn't care if I'm in there since I'm not in the habit of wrecking things. He has stuff in his room that I like to play with, and vice versa.

I could sleep in there if I wanted, she wouldn't care. No one's going to stop me.

Still, instead of going in and trying to figure out what's going on, I've been sitting on the couch, doing nothing. It's been days now. I've spent hours sitting here, not taking action.

All the while I'm thinking about that stupid, plastic block.

I know the batteries are out, I know it's not going to glow, and I'd like to take a closer look at it. But darn it, I'm nervous!

"Jed, doodle! Where are you?" I hear my mom calling me and snap out of my couch induced lassitude.

Ty's laying at my feet, legs sticking straight up in the air, mouth hanging open, tongue lolling as he snores. At her call, he jumps up, loses his balance and goes toppling over the edge of the couch, onto the floor.

"That was graceful, Ty, very nice."

He cocks his head, listening to me, then dismisses my words with a huff. He walks away, heading to where my mom is coming from, ready to intercept her.

I know he's thinking she might have some food for him, pig.

"I'm in the living room, mom! And PLEASE stop calling me that!"

I hear her padding through the house. It's cold, so she wears these crazy pink socks with rubber traction on the bottom. I think they're actually intended for hospital patients, but she likes them, and she's my mom, so I don't judge.

She walks up to the back of the couch and leans a hip on it. Then she reaches out and ruffles my hair.

I really don't like it when she does that, but I don't have the heart to tell her.

Looking down at me, she starts picking up all the trash I've piled on the couch edge. An empty bag of chips, a cup that had water in it, a tissue.

Don't make that face, I have snot sometimes!

Also, I'm kind of a slob, it's not just Thomas.

"Hey bug, I just talked to your dad." she begins, but I interrupt her. "Mom, I'm 10, you have got to stop calling me nicknames like that."

"Aww, sorry bug, I mean, Jed," she says. "I'll try to remember." She ruffles my hair again, balancing my trash in a pile in her other hand.

She starts to walk back to the kitchen, no doubt to clean up my mess. I worry that she's forgotten what she was going to say to me.

It happens!

"Anyhow", I get us back on topic, "You talked to dad? I thought he and Thomas were going to be out of cell phone range all week."

I feel some emotion knowing that she was able to talk to dad and Thomas. It feels sort of like excitement, but also sort of like dread.

I'm going to call it anxious.

Yeah, it makes me anxious, that's a great word!

"Well, yes, they are out of range," she says, turning back toward me. "but your dad says that when he's in a certain field, he can stand on top of the Gator and get some reception. So he called to let us know that they got there safely, and they're having fun."

She disappears from view as she bends down behind the bar. I hear her open the cabinet door to put my stuff in the garbage can.

"Oh, okay, awesome," I say, sitting up straighter, trying to catch her eye so I can ask if Thomas said anything else.

There's no need though, apparently, he did say something else.

"Listen, honey," she stands back up and leans on the counter, "your brother asked your dad to give you a message. Something about a game he wants you to try. It's called....Zombie Assault, or Rescue something....."

"Rescue Mission: Zombie Assault!" I end up yelling it because suddenly, I have a clue!!

I'm definitely not yelling it because I'm excited to go in there, that's even worse than the last place I went.

Mom looks at me like I've lost my mind a little bit.

I get slowly up from the couch, limp over to the kitchen, and give her a quick hug. I take the dishes from her hand and start loading them in the dishwasher. "Thanks, mom, I've been thinking about trying that game. I'm going to go check it out."

"Okay, sweetie, have fun. Stay off that ankle, though." She glances pointedly at my bandage wrapped foot, looks back at me, then pads off on those silly socks.....

All of the sudden, my day has a little more purpose. I have a starting point now. It's not ideal, I don't like the thought of joining a game about zombies, but nothing says I have to go inside of it.

I can just log in and see if maybe Thomas somehow left me a message. Perhaps he told Kat or Jake to meet me in there so we could chat.

Either way, it's nice to think that Thomas knows a little bit about what happened.

It's nice not to feel so alone.

CHAPTER 3

BUSTED ANKLES
AND YOUTUBERS

Before I go any further, I think you might have some questions. At least, if I were the one outside the story, I'd have questions right now.

The game I got pulled into was about prisoners trying to escape their cells, rob banks, and wreak havoc in town.

The game I'm about to log into is about zombies. More specifically it's about zombies invading an island.

The people on the island try to get rescued by a person flying a helicopter. If they get rescued, they get flown to a carrier. Once there, they can get their own helicopter and go save more people.

The two games don't have anything in common. Is that what you were thinking?

You're right, they don't.

If you better understand Roblox, you'll better understand why these two are going to be so different.

Basically, Roblox is just a hub, a sort of space on the internet where people go and build their own worlds. It's been around awhile, probably longer than I've been alive actually.

There are thousands of worlds, maybe tens of thousands, but it's all accessed from the main website.

Does that make sense?

One minute you could play a prison game, the next you can fight zombies.

You could even go have a dance off and kill people who don't know the right songs.

The possibilities are endless.

I put my palm on the arm of the couch and ease my way up to a standing position so I can hobble down the hall to my bedroom. I'm going slowly but trying to get there before my mom sees me and makes me use the stupid crutch she bought online.

Walking with a crutch sucks, probably even more than having a sprained ankle sucks.

This makes me think of something else I wanted to tell you.

I don't know if you can bring things into the game when you travel through the portal, but I doubt it (more on that later). What I do know for sure is that if something terrible happens to you while you're there, you'll bring it out with you.

If you get out, that is.

By the same token, I'm not entirely sure if you can bring THINGS out with you, but I sort of doubt it.

Here's why.

When I hit my head on that block the other night, I was wearing pajamas and carrying my iPad. When I woke up in the game, I was wearing prison-issued clothing and carrying nothing at all.

Also, remember the wall I jumped off while escaping the prison grounds? I landed badly and messed up my ankle. When Ty dragged me back through the portal, I was no longer wearing prison-issue clothes, but my ankle was still sprained and bruised. It was swollen to the size of a softball, and very much injured. Same with the shrapnel cuts on my face, though they are a lot less noticeable.

I had to think of something to tell my mom. That was the toughest part, really.

I ended up telling her that I fell while I was playing "war" in the yard. That game always involves a lot of jumping, rolling, and dodging, plenty of ways to injure myself.

My explanation was short, sweet, and entirely believable. She didn't question it, but

I do need to be careful. After all, there are only so many injuries a guy can explain away.

Anyhow, she took me to the doctor, he confirmed it was just a sprain, but I do need to stay off of it for a bit.

Hopefully, I can log onto the zombie game and get some answers without actually having to go back into the game. I can't imagine trying to escape flesh-eating monsters while hobbling around on one foot.

#nosir

I smile as I make my way to my room, eyes lingering on the picture of Thomas and I skiing in Colorado.

Despite the pain in my foot and the uncertainty I'm feeling, I'm glad Thomas left me a message. It feels like some sort of acceptance, like we're in this together.

It's been so long since he and I have been in anything together.

It's a huge relief, even if it isn't in the manner I was hoping for. One way or another, I've got my brother back, and that makes me happy.

I'd think if he wanted to keep me out of it altogether, he'd act like nothing ever happened, right? He's been denying that anything odd has been going on for months now, so why stop?

It would be easy enough for him to act like I had a bad dream or something. It's not like I'd have any way to prove otherwise.

This message has to mean something.

He's not just telling me about it, he's going far enough to direct me to another world.

I can only think that he wants my help.

Maybe whatever it is he needs me to do has to be done right now. Perhaps it can't wait the four days until he gets back, so he's trusting me to take care of it.

I wish I could ask him.

I can't though, so I'll do the next best thing.

In my room, I get ready to play.

My computer is already set up, facing away from my window, so I don't get any glare.

I have my mouse and an excellent mouse pad that's supposed to make my movements even more exact.

My desk and chair are adjustable, so I move both to make room for my leg, which I have to prop up on another chair.

Thomas and I have exactly the same types of desks, only different colors. His is blue, mine is grey. I needed an extra chair for my foot, so I asked mom, and she went to his room and brought his chair to me.

Now it's a footstool.

She even put a little pillow on it, just to make sure I'm comfortable.

It's like poetic justice. There's no reason I shouldn't be resting my foot in his chair.

After all, I maintain that it's his fault I have an injured foot in the first place.

I wiggle my mouse to wake my computer, looking at the laptop wallpaper screen that shows a snarling wolf standing on a rock outcropping. "Be fierce, Jed," I think to myself.

The website is already up, no surprise since it's the website I'm on 99% of the time if I'm on my laptop.

I do have an iPad, and you can play Roblox that way, but only some of the worlds work.

All of the worlds work if you're on the computer.

I don't even have to log in. My computer asked me a long time ago if I wanted to save the password permanently, and I totally said yes.

#dontjudge

I have about a billion different passwords for the things I do online. Mom even has a list of them hanging on the refrigerator so she can figure them out when I forget what they are.

It happens more often than I'd like to admit.

It's the bane of the digital age! She always complains: "Things weren't like this when I was a kid. We had a console video game that didn't even remember your progress, let alone ask you to log in!"

I'm not sure why she gets on to me about it. I'm not the one who invented the internet, and I know she likes it as much as I do, so.....

Side note:

Does your mom think it's downright odd that you have favorite YouTubers?

Mine does!

If she wants to watch something, she turns on Netflix. She doesn't get the hype behind DanTDM, Papa Jake, and my current favorite JackPlaysStuff. I've tried to explain it, but what can I say, she just doesn't understand.

Anyway, the reason I thought about it was that one of those guys made a video about this game a few weeks back.

I've played it once or twice, it's kind of stressful.

It sounds easy enough, but I've watched that video. I saw how many different helicopters came.

I also saw how many got destroyed before he finally got rescued.

Apparently, the zombies can kill the pilot, or the helicopter can crash into the ocean, etc.

Basically, the game is perilous.

Am I really doing this?

CHAPTER 4

YOU'VE GOT MAIL
BUT YOU MIGHT NOT WANT IT

The red dot on my game chat is lit up when I log in.

No surprise there.

I've been playing for a couple of years, so I've got a lot of online friends.

#popular

My friend's list shows me if any of them have sent me messages. It also shows me which ones have invited me to play, and which games they're in right now.

What does surprise me is that I have a message request from someone who has also requested me as a friend.

"Katastrophe1721 has sent you a friend request," I read aloud.

There's a quick rush of excitement, followed by a more prolonged rush of....I'm not sure, dread, anxiety?

What's the word for when you feel like you want to cheer and puke all in the same minute?

That word. That's how I feel.

It was what I wanted, right? I mean just this morning I was trying to figure out how to get ahold of her. Well, here she is, messaging me, just like she promised she would.

The anxiety comes from knowing that if I accept that friend request and/or read that message, there's no going back.

I'm at a crossroads right now. I've been in the game, yes, but that doesn't mean I have to have anything else to do with whatever this is.

Even if I don't know HOW I know, I'm sure that me ending up in that game was a big deal to Kat and Jake. They were scared for me, scared of whoever was after me.

I sit there, staring at the screen, making sure this is what I really want to do, what I really SHOULD do.

The decision is made though. If I weren't going to commit myself to finding out what's going on, I'd have put it out of my mind. I'd have pretended like it never happened.

My mouse hovers over "Accept Request".

Click

It's done.

I wait, but nothing happens.

I guess I was thinking something would happen.

Like *poof* I'm friends with Kat, and therefore I will know everything about everything!

What a letdown.

Undeterred, I click over to my chat messages.

Now that we're friends, I can see the message she sent me. Maybe she answers some questions there.

Katastrophe1721 - "Jed, meet me tonight, 6 p.m. RM:ZA, the cave by the base. Kat."

That's it?

I scroll up and down, but nope, that's it.

I guess I was expecting a little more. I thought she'd say "Hey Jed, I hope you're okay, I hope you didn't die, and that your foot is better. It was my fault you got into this in the first place, I owe you a solid. Also, sorry I made you crawl through poop."

Maybe not exactly like that, but something?

Points to her for being concise, I guess...

Well, it's easy enough to interpret anyway, there's that.

According to her....brief note, I'm going to meet her in the game this evening.

By "in the game", I mean me sitting here AT MY COMPUTER, with my busted ankle kicked up (gently) while I relax in my chair.

In the meantime, I decide to join Zombie Assault. I figure I can get a lay of the land and make sure I know exactly where she wants to meet.

Actually, I think I'll head over to the cave and then log out. That way, when I log back in, I'll be right there!

Sometimes I impress myself with my forethought, truly!

The load screen comes up, and my character appears on the island.

It's pretty dull as far as islands go, big and green, lots of trees, you get the idea. I run a little way and the zombies materialize, ready to make me their next meal.

I know I'm going to have to fight my way to this cave (which I've never seen before, so it might take some doing), so I pull up my inventory and find a suitable weapon.

Generally, I like to go with a good old-fashioned automatic rifle. Lots of bullets mean an easy kill from a distance.

The further I am away from their teeth, the better.

My inventory looks like a set of cubicles, 4 across, 4 down, for a total of 16 slots in the bag. I usually have like 10 weapons, some food, water, and a bandage or two.

This time though, I notice three items that were not in there the last time I played.

First, there is a small, blue bottle.

It's clear, with a brown stopper, like a cork? It actually looks a whole lot like the potion bottles you see in Minecraft, but I've never seen one in this game.

I hover over it, but as soon as my cursor moves over the bottle, it greys out. No amount of clicking will let me read the description, equip it, or use it.

That's a bit frustrating, so I try to drag it out of my inventory, off the screen, trashing it. No dice, I can't touch it, must be a glitch. I tell myself that I'll deal with it later on.

Chances are if it is a glitch, the game makers will deal with it before I need to.

Second, there's a small stone, it looks like a skipping stone, grey, flat, with a blue swirl in the middle.

I hover over it, but can't do anything with it, same as the bottle, so I just ignore it.

They must be doing an update or something.

Third, there's a map, it's tiny, a lot like the map in Minecraft.

How odd.

I click on it, and this time I actually CAN click on it. WOO HOO!

The map pops up. It shows the island. Different colored dots indicate where I am, where the base is, there's even a little ship in the ocean that must be the carrier.

Near the base, there is a small black mark that looks sort of like an upside down half moon.

That could definitely be a cave.
Time to find out.

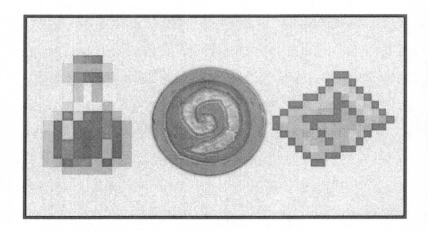

CHAPTER 5

BRUH....

Getting to the half moon mark on the map should be a pretty straightforward process.

I've been "near" the area at least a dozen times, but I've never noticed the cave.

It's understandable. When you're being attacked by 50 zombies and trying to board a helicopter, you tend to get a little bit of tunnel vision.

Players are running all over the place, either from zombies or toward them. The zombies amble around, either in small packs or by themselves, and the whole game feels a bit chaotic.

Nothing new there.

I'm running over the grass, sliding down small hills, swinging from trees, and dodging the single-minded undead, shooting them when I can't avoid them. Amidst this noise, I hear the familiar "chop chop chop" of a helicopter.

Huh.

That's not really unusual, I mean the helicopters are an integral part of the game. They're flying around, trying to pick up other players to get them to safety. If they succeed, they can bring the player back to a carrier that's stationed out in the ocean.

Some players are here on the island killing zombies. Others have killed the zombies and made it back to base. Some of those hitch a chopper ride and grab their own chopper to make their own rescues.

It's like the life cycle of a frog, or evaporation, only in a video game.

The thing that is odd is that I'm not actually anywhere near the base. There are miles of the island between where I spawn and where I need to be to get picked up.

The pickup point looks like the turret of a castle. It butts up to the water. Zombies don't swim all that often, so it's easier for a player to stand with their back to the water, shooting toward the land.

The pilots can land either on the base or on the sand, but the whole process is a lot easier if you're only having to keep a look out in front of you.

If a pilot tries to pick someone up where I'm standing right now, we'd face zombies from all sides.

A rescue would be practically impossible.

Here I am though, in the middle of a field, zig-zagging my way through mobs, and watching a helicopter hover above me. At first, I think he might be trying to pick me up, so I stop and wait, but he makes no move to land.

The zombies come at me, and I'm forced to run again, but the chopper keeps pace.

I toggle my screen, letting my character gaze toward the sky. The sun is blazing overhead, making it hard to see anything except the dark outline of the helicopter.

I shrug in my seat, dismissing it.

Pop! Pop! Pop!

My character dies, arms, head, and legs exploding off my body.

The guy who killed me didn't do anything special, that's just how you die in Roblox.

This makes no sense. Why did that guy shoot me? Doesn't he know how to play?

As far as I know, zombies aren't able to fly helicopters, so it's highly unlikely one of them shot me.

I chalk it up to a noob kid having some fun, click the button to let my character respawn, and continue running toward the mark on the map.

Not 25 feet later, it happens again.

Pop! Pop! Pop! Pop!

Son of a gun! What is going on?!

Players aren't supposed to kill other players in this game! Just like helicopters sure aren't the choice of weapon when you're trying to take out a group of zombies!

I'm dead again, fun.

This time, because it's so soon after I died the first time, I have to wait to respawn.

The timer starts at 30 seconds, and I just sit there while it counts down, staring at my ceiling and the little stars my parents stuck to it.

They glow at night, it's cool.

The stars, not my parents.

At this rate, I am never going to make it to the cave. I'm not sure what joker of a kid thinks this is hilarious, but they're really getting on my nerves.

The timer finishes, I click the button, and my character appears on the screen.

I toggle my mouse to look up at the helicopter again. I'm going to get this kid's name and give him a piece of my mind!

Before I can make out the player's name, I hear a *ping* and see that I have an in-game "whisper".

Another player is making contact with me. I look down at the message bar.

"So close, and yet so far, eh Jed?"

I freeze in my chair, adrenaline courses through my veins, keeping me rooted to the spot.

My heart starts beating fast in my chest, my mouth goes dry, and I get prickly and sweaty in my armpits.

Those were the exact words he said to me the last time I saw him, three days ago, when he was trying to keep me from getting home.

It's Dirk.

CHAPTER 6

MyNameIsJed
This Could Be A Katastrophe

I didn't bother responding to Dirk's whisper. I didn't even really consider responding. What would I say?

I don't want to talk to the guy. Part of me was hoping I'd never see him again.

I don't know why I thought that would happen.

He knew who I was in the game, as much as Kat and Jake knew who I was. Common sense should have told me that he is as much a part of...whatever this is, as I am, as any of us are.

Once he messaged me, I logged out. I didn't continue trying to get to the cave, I didn't do anything. I just turned off the game and sat there.

Eventually, my heart stopped racing, and it left me feeling exhausted. I slumped back against the grey plastic back of my chair, shoulders hunched, head hanging toward the floor.

I feel sick thinking of that small interaction. How did he track me? How did he know I was on? I'm not friends with the guy, so how did he know?

Was I wrong to come here? It's not too late to turn back. If I never meet Kat at the cave, it's not like she can force me in, right?

I raise my eyes to the ceiling, mouthing "I hope I'm right."

Is this what happened to Thomas? Did he stumble into this thing, and just hasn't been able to find a way out? Or is this thing so big that he doesn't want out?

Is he trying to help someone?

If I had two good ankles, I'd have worn a hole in the floor from pacing. As it was, I sat in my computer chair, mind blanking out, staring at the screen until Mom came in and told me that lunch was ready.

She's worried about me, I can tell. Ankle issue aside, she's got that "Mom sense" thing going on.

"Jed, everything okay?" She kneels down next to my chair on the blue rug in my room, getting at eye level. "You seem like you've been a little off the past few days. Are you feeling alright?"

She puts her hand on my forehead, checking for fever in the way parents do.

At least she doesn't put her lips on my forehead anymore. That was embarrassing from the moment I realized what embarrassment was.

"I'm fine, mom." I look up at her and find my stomach giving a little lurch. What if I hadn't gotten back here? Would I have ever seen her again?

I can feel my eyes welling up a bit, so I duck my head and fiddle with my computer, blinking rapidly. "It's just the server is down, so I was waiting for it to come back up."

"Oh, okay," she says, rubbing her hand gently over my hair, but I can tell she's not convinced, "well lunch is ready, so come on before it gets cold."

She stands, then leans down to help me up out of the chair. I hold on to her arm as we walk into the kitchen, enjoying her warmth.

Food getting cold is a real concern these days, truth! The temperature outside is making the heater run continually. Despite this, things left on our white IKEA table still get cold super, quick!

I eat my sandwich, being quiet and thinking serious thoughts. Mom is having soup while reading her Kindle.

It's how we roll.

After we're done, I figured I might as well catch up on my homework, then Mom asked if I wanted to watch a movie with her.

We love watching movies together, and if that makes me lame, then I don't want to be...not lame. Whatever the opposite of lame is. The opposite of lame is NOT "The Emoji Movie" just so you know. #thatmoviewasbad

It's 5:58 now. I'm sitting at my desk, trying to be as chill as I can.

I'm logged back into Roblox, but not back into the world I'm supposed to be in. I can kid myself and say that it's because I just want to wait until 6:00, but we both know that's not true.

I'm a little sick with the thought that as soon as I log back in, Dirk will be there, trying to kill me.

The clock ticks over another minute 5:59.

"Okay, Jed. It's now or never," I tell myself, shrugging my shoulders, loosening up, trying to calm my nerves, "just deal and do what you need to do."

My pep talk doesn't work, I don't feel any PEPPIER, but I know there's only one thing to be done.

I hover over the "Join" button and *click* just as a message comes through my chat.

Katastrophe1721 - *Use the stone.*

MyNameIsJed - What?

Katastrophe1721 - *Once you get in the game, use the stone in your inventory.*

Oh! So she put that stuff in my inventory?

It makes sense. She was trying to help me find the cave by giving me the map, and I guess I'm about to figure out what the stone is for.

I'll have to ask her about the potion once I've used the stone.

The game finishes its loading screen. My computer displays my character.

I see that I'm standing on the island in the same place I was when Dirk last killed me. It's been a few hours. I don't immediately hear the chop of a helicopter, but I'm not sticking around to find out if he's still around.

I move my wrist, putting the cursor over the button that brings up my inventory, then I hover over the previously unusable grey stone.

My cursor (it looks like a little hand in a metal gauntlet) turns white, indicating the item can now be used.

Perfect.

As soon as I click it, a thin, hollow bar appears at the bottom of my screen.

It's a timer, going from empty to full as the stone glows and pulses in my inventory slot. I'd say it takes about 15 seconds to fill entirely with blue, and then when the bar is full, my screen fades out.

I can't do anything, it's another loading screen just like what I see when I travel from one world to the next.

I sit there and wait, but since I have a pretty good computer, it doesn't take very long for my screen to come back up.

The black blurs into pixels, and the pixels turn into crisp pictures.

I'm in a cave, which is actually what I expected. It's dark, the dominant colors being brown and black, shot through with the bright orange of a fire.

I'm in the middle of the space, and it's quite large. You could fit 20 of me side by side, and I can't even see the ceiling, so I have no idea how far up it goes.

It's just dark up there, nothing but shadows.

This isn't a place I've ever been in the game, which is also what I expected.

I use my mouse to change my view, looking up and down, side to side. I don't see any holes to fall into or mobs that might eat me, so I use my "A W S D" keys to move around and check it out.

It's awesome looking!

There are torches on the walls that give off most of the light, and a fire in the middle. The fire is surrounded by stones, like something a conscientious camper would build.

There is bedding laid out around the fire. I see a rack holding rifles and ammunition propped against one of the cave walls.

There's even a vendor in here! I run over to him to see if he sells anything I might use, but he's just got the usual stuff, some junk weapons, a bit of food, that sort of thing.

What the heck, it's still totally cool.

As far as I can tell, there's no way in, and no way out. I guess that stone was a sort of beacon or homing device? How have I never heard of this place?

I'm walking around the cave when I hear footsteps behind me. I whirl, expecting to see Dirk, but it's just Kat.

Katastrophe1721 - *Hey, captain observant.*

MyNameIsJed - I knew you were there.

Really, I didn't, but I will never give her the satisfaction of saying so.

I take a moment to look at her, clicking on her person and checking out her gear. She has some fantastic stuff, stuff I've never even heard of.

Her little digital character looks nothing like the "real" her I met in the game a few nights ago.

If that was the real her....

I move my character to face her and jump up and down to get her attention again.

MyNameIsJed - *Soooooo, hey.*

Katastrophe1721 - Put on your headset.

MyNameIsJed - *What?*

Katastrophe1721 - It's easier to talk if we don't have to type.

Oooh, of course! That makes total sense.

Typing isn't my strong suit, anyhow. Being able to talk in Discord will make this way better.

I grab the headset that's hanging from a small metal "u" shaped peg on the side of my desk and slip it over my ears. I push the adaptor into my computer and hold down my right mouse key so she can hear me talk.

There is an option that keeps my microphone on always, but I'd rather not do that.

A guy needs a little privacy.

"Can you hear me?" I test the microphone once I have everything set up.

Her voice crackles through cyberspace, "Hey Jed, yep, I can hear you. Thanks for coming!"

She sounds so happy that I'm here. Was she thinking I wouldn't show up?

I don't blame her. I almost didn't show up.

"Sure thing. I mean I'm not really sure what you wanted me for, but I know I have some questions for you, so maybe you can fill me in a bit?"

If she's going to ask me to do something, and I have a feeling she is, then I'm going to get my answers first. No more stalling.

"I will, as much as I can, at least," she replies. "I can't do it like this though, I need you to meet me here, back in Roblox."

You know how something happens and you're sort of waiting for the other shoe to drop? This was my other shoe. I knew this meeting would be about me going back into the game.

I knew it.

Part of me is excited to do it, the other part of me is totally not excited.

What if I don't come back, what if I don't make it out of the portal in time?

Is that how I'll get in and out? Are there portals everywhere, or is Kat controlling them?

So many questions.

I decide that I've got to get some answers before I agree to anything. It's just the smart thing to do.

Sitting back in my chair, I rub my hands over my buzz cut hair and think about what I most want to know.

"You there, Jed?" No doubt she's wondering if I've bailed.

I tap my fingers on my knee in a rapid motion. Thumb, first finger, middle finger, ring finger, pinky finger, then back again.

"Brrrrap brrrap brrrap" the noise makes me realize how agitated I am at the thought of doing this.

"How would I get there?"

I have more questions, she's going to have to sit here and take the time to answer them before I agree to anything.

I ask two more questions in rapid succession. "How would I get back home? It was a near thing last time, how do I know this time I'd actually make it?"

These are the things I need to know before I can decide if I'll go back in.

"There's a portal here, in this game," Kat tells me. "That's part of why I need you. If you come, we can close down the portal, we can seal off the game so that no one else can make the Jump."

"The Jump?" I capitalize it in my head because it sounds like that's what she's doing.

She's not talking about hopping up and down. "What are you talking about?"

"We're Jumpers, people like me, you, Jake, Thomas.....Dirk."

I cut her off, using my one good leg to kick my chair back, so it's balancing only on the back feet.

"Wait, speaking of Dirk, that guy was in the game today when I came on. I was going to try to find the cave so I wouldn't have to walk all the way over here when it was time to meet you."

I guess if I'd known what the stone did, I could have saved myself some trouble.

"Dirk was here?" Her voice gets tight. "I'm sorry, Jed. I didn't think he'd find you this fast."

"How did he find me at all? How is that even possible?"

I can feel myself getting mad, so I sit my chair back down, shut my eyes and move my head from side to side, touching my shoulders with my ears, working out the kinks.

"Is he some type of hacker or something? Does he know who I am now?"

She's silent for a minute.

"Yes and no," she says, "he has....abilities in Roblox. Rather, he knows people with abilities, people who can get him information. All he needed was your username anyway, he can find you whenever he wants."

"We're not friends though!" I shout it, then check myself. I don't want my mom to come in. "We're not friends. How can he see me if he and I aren't friends?"

"You don't have to be friends with him. He's friends with people high enough in the game that he can always find out where you are." She sighs. It's a solemn sound, and I know she's worried that I'm not going to help her.

"People high enough in what game, in Zombie Rush?"

"No," she replies, "people high enough in Roblox."

"You're talking the whole site, the whole website, the people who created it, he knows them?"

That's crazy, it's illegal for sure. They can't just give out my information!

"Yes, that's what I'm saying."

I think she's going to stop talking, but she pushes on.

"Jed, I know this freaks you out, and I'm sorry for it, but this is why I need you. The damage is done, they know you exist."

I feel like I know what's coming, and I don't want to hear it.

"They know where you are now. Whether you come back in and help me or not, you're on their radar." She stops, then starts again. "At least if you come back in, we can try to stop them together."

As far as reasons go, it's actually pretty compelling.

"I don't understand, Kat." I continue to hold my "talk" button down so she can't interrupt me. "None of this makes any sense. It's like you're telling me there's some giant conspiracy in this game, and we're all unwitting victims."

"I know, Jed. And that's why I need you to come. Meet me in the game, let me explain, and if you decide you want to help us, great. If not, I'll help you get to the portal, and you can go home."

There's a small pause as she chooses her next words.

"I don't know how much good it will do you if you decide not to join us. I don't think they'll give up on finding you, but I promise to give you a choice. At least give me a chance to show you, though. A chance to explain."

"Everything, Kat," I say, "if I "Jump" again, you have to tell me everything."

I'm not backing down on this, I want answers.

"Okay, Jed. I'll tell you everything, I promise."

And just like that, I know I'm headed back into Zombie Assault.

CHAPTER 7

IF I'M NOT BACK IN 5 MINUTES.....

"You're going to need the Redstone Block," Kat tells me.

I slide my chair away from my desk, reach up to take off my headset, type "AFK" into the chat bar, and hobble slowly to Thomas's room.

I keep my eyes peeled because I know if my mom sees me, she's going to accost me with that crutch, forcing me to use it.

I really hate that crutch!

Ty is already in Thomas's room laying on his bed, sleeping the day away. He raises his head and looks at me, brown eyes blinking slowly.

No doubt I'm committing the ultimate crime, disturbing his slumber.

"I'll be in and out, your majesty." I pat his great big head and scratch his ears.

He groans then rolls over on his back and digs his nose into Thomas's pillow.

"Yuck," I mumble. It cannot be pleasant to sleep on dried dog drool....

The Redstone Block is still on the floor, lying in pieces, right where I flung it. I pick up the box, the panel, and the two AA batteries that power the stupid thing. I make sure to look down at the floor this time as I leave, not wanting to repeat my mistake from 3 days ago.

This time I step around that stupid piece of yellow chalk.

I shuffle back to my room, easing down the hallway, holding the block out in front of me like it's a poisonous snake. I make it back to my desk and sit down, putting my headset on again.

The ear covers crackle with static cling as they slide over my head. I click my talk button and let Kat know that I'm back.

Looking at the block, I frown. There's no way I'm putting it together right now, it's staying in pieces until absolutely necessary. I'm not sure what to do with it though, so I set it on my shelf in a little pile of parts.

"Alright," I say, "I've got it, what do you want me to do with it?"

"Just put the batteries back in," she starts, but I cut her off.

"Nope, not gonna happen until I need to use it. That thing is dangerous."

"It's not dangerous, Jed." She sighs, and I can just imagine her rolling her eyes. "I was going to say that you just need to put the batteries back in before it'll work, so do that only when you're ready to go."

I grit my teeth but say nothing. I feel like she's taking this whole Redstone Block thing too lightly. Clearly, she's been around the block (no pun intended) more than me, so I'll keep an open mind, for now.

"Alright, but listen, I can't do this right now," I tell her. "My mom doesn't go to sleep until 10 or so, which means I have to act normal until then. How much time is this going to take? Can I meet you back here at like 10:30?"

I'm grateful that it's the weekend; otherwise my internet time would cut off a lot earlier. If that were the case, I wouldn't be able to do this at all.

"Yeah, that's fine. I need a little time to get everything ready anyway. I'll see you at 10:30. Log in to the game, check your inventory, and follow the directions."

I log off, I guess I'll see her, in person, in a few hours.

CHAPTER 8

THOMAS CAN BE DUMB IT'S FUNNY

The rest of the evening passes normally. At least as normal as it can be with me knowing I'll be in a zombie-filled wasteland tonight.

It makes you appreciate the little things, you know?

Mom and I eat dinner, then we watch an episode of "Father Brown". It's a pretty good murder mystery show if you like that stuff.

I'm off my game tonight though, I can't even figure out who the killer is before Father Brown does.

This zombie thing is affecting me!

After the show is over, mom stands up and starts making her way around the living room.

She's always clearing up before she goes to bed. Actually, she's always clearing up. I guess I'm messy, a bit.

I help her with the dishes, and she gives me a long look. She knows something's up, I never help with the dishes.

I pretend not to notice her stare, finish putting the dishes in the dishwasher, and give her a hug.

"Night Mom, I love you," I tell her.

I start toward my room, but she stops me with a hand on my shoulder. "I love you, too, Jed. If you want to talk about anything, I'm here."

"I know, mom."

Maybe I will talk to her, if I can't handle things, maybe.

In my room, I lay on my back on my twin bed, staring up at the ceiling. The beige walls are covered in my artwork. Drawings I've done over the last 10 years, pictures of places we've been as a family.

Everything on these walls reminds me of all that I love.

My stomach is in knots.

Do I really want to do this again? At least the first time I Jumped, it wasn't on purpose. But this time? If something goes wrong, it'll be my fault, because I could have said no.

What on earth am I thinking?

Then I remember what Kat said tonight. Something about how "they" might leave me alone if I stay out of the game, but that she doubted it.

Isn't it better for me to be proactive about this? Isn't it better that I get as much information as I can?

I think it is.

I think Thomas wouldn't be Jumping into a video game without good reason. He certainly wouldn't do it if he thought he wouldn't be able to make it home.

So either what he's doing is really important, or he's a whole lot dumber than I thought!

That makes me laugh to myself.

Thomas really does some stupid things now and then.

There was that time he skidded on some wet leaves and drove his dirt bike straight into a fence. My mom was sprinting toward what I'm sure she thought was his unconscious body, when he picked his helmeted up off the grass and gave a "Thumbs Up."

Another time, he shot my grandmother's chicken with a bb gun, it died, and dad made him bring it home and eat it for dinner.

I thought he'd never get off grounding!

Then there was the time he found a hand-drawn portrait of my grandfather at my grandparents house. My grandmother was going to have it framed, so she'd left it on the table. He took it outside, taped it to a light pole, and wrote "WANTED" across it.

Sometimes, I'm amazed he's lived to 12.

Okay, so no, I don't think Thomas would do it if it weren't important.

I use that thought to steel myself for what's to come. If he can do it, I can do it.

There's no way he'd give me the message about the video game if he didn't WANT me to keep going, if he didn't think I was capable.

That thought, more than anything else, seals the deal for me.

Thomas would NOT give me this information if he didn't think it was essential AND he didn't think I could handle it.

He wouldn't send me someplace that had a high chance of getting me killed.

He must think I'm wily enough to control things, or smart enough not to get caught.

I AM smart enough not to get caught, especially now that I won't be taken by surprise.

I roll over, lean up on one elbow, and grab the Redstone Block pieces from my shelf. Then I push myself up into a sitting position on my bed and hobble to my computer chair, logging back in.

The screen comes up quickly, as though it can sense my urgency to get this over with.

I join the zombie game, and when I'm loaded in the first thing I do is hover my mouse over my inventory.

Of the original three items Kat put in there, only the potion bottle remains.

There are two new things though, and I hover over both, checking them out.

First, there is a note icon that looks like an unopened envelope. I click it.

A message pops up on my screen:

"Jed, when you're ready, put the block back together. Turn the switch to the "On"

position, and tap the block 3 times. Be sure to place it where you don't mind coming back out of the portal."

Second, there is a Redstone Block. It looks just like the one Thomas got for Christmas.

I sit there a second, looking at it, unsure of whether I even want to try to hover over it, but I do.

It's grey, I can't do anything, and I am relieved!

Well, I guess it's time to put the block back together. I knew I couldn't avoid it forever.

I pick it up and begin sliding the batteries in and securing the panel. I don't turn it on though, I want to make sure I've got everything ready first.

I remember the last time I went in. None of my clothes transferred over (I was in prison-issued garb when I woke up), but I didn't try to BRING anything with me.

I thought I was holding my iPad when I tripped and hit my head, but what if I dropped it before I hit my head? It's been nagging at me, not being sure about that part of things.

This time, I'm going to hold on to something, and then I'll know whether bringing stuff in is a possibility.

I look around the room, deciding what to take. The iPad really is too big, and I don't have a phone yet.....but Thomas does.

Another long trip to his room (man this busted foot is no fun) and back, and I've got an iPhone in hand. If it comes through, great, I can use it to take pictures.

If not, well...not great, but at least I'll know.

Now, where do I want to put the block to make sure I can get back alright?

I'm not sure I want to put it on the floor. Not that I think anyone will mess with it, if they did it would really be the least of my problems.

I'm also not sure if it'll stop me from getting out if the block is on a shelf.

Not a chance I want to take. I settle for laying it on my pillow, placing it down reverently like it's a bomb that might explode at any moment.

tick tick tick

I make sure I've got socks, shoes, jeans, a warm sweater, a jacket, and the iPhone. Not because I think the clothes will transfer, not really.

It's just that I cannot imagine wearing only my pajamas and showing up on the island in boxer shorts.

If ever there was a moment when clothes would Jump with me, this would be it.

The last thing I need is to get ripped up by thick grass, rocks, and trees while I stumble through the game in bare feet.

Ty pads into my room after me. He sits down, scratches behind his ear in that energetic way dogs do, then looks at me expectantly.

"Okay, hang on," I tell him, knowing exactly what he wants.

I hop over to my bed, pick up the books and iPad off the cover and place them on my shelf. Ty huffs then jumps up on the blanket. He circles a few times, apparently satisfied with all the room he now has to stretch out, and plops down.

He's a creature who loves his creature comforts, so I just let him be.

I take back what I said about Thomas sleeping on dog drool. Apparently, I do it, too.

"Wish me luck, Tyrone." I give him a quick scratch between his ears, he licks my hand, then goes back to sleep, paws already starting to twitch as he dreams.

I pick up the Redstone Block, flip the switch to "On", and set it back down on the bed, well away from Ty's head.

No time like the present. I place my hand over the block, holding it there for a second, bracing myself for what's to come.

I bring my hand down.

Tap

The light turns on dim.

Tap

The light gets a little brighter.

Tap

My world goes black.

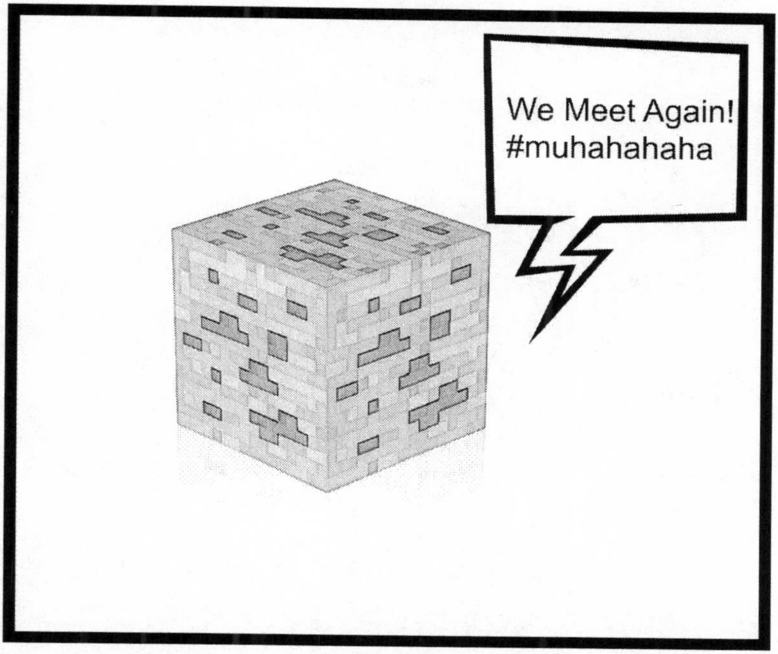
We Meet Again!
#muhahahaha

CHAPTER 9

 DIRT FLOORS AND BAD CATS

I wake up in a cave, or rather "the cave", the one I logged out in a few hours ago. I expected as much, but man, it's not fun when you're a real person, not nearly as cool.

As soon as I open my eyes, I start shivering. Do none of these games have any settings other than "meat locker"?

The ground I'm laying on is damp and cold. Apparently, the bedding I saw earlier is more for looks and not so much for me actually putting my back on.

I take a deep breath, preparing to ask Kat why she couldn't have planned this a little better.

Instead of talking, I sneeze. So, in addition to it being cold and damp, it's also musty, and it smells like the inside of a wet shoe.

Yay!

I roll over and sit up.

No prison mattress for me this time, nope.

I never thought I'd be all "Well at least I could have a mattress like I did in that prison game." And yet, here I am, thinking those exact thoughts.

All that's under me is dirt, rocks, and sticks. Scratch that. I look around. All that's anywhere is dirt, rocks, and sticks.

I'm wearing only what my character has on in Roblox, none of my stuff came over with me.

There's that question answered at least.

My outfit consists of beige pants, a green short sleeve shirt, and brown shoes.

One of the shoes is way too tight on my injured foot, and there is a black cat sitting on my shoulder.

Oh man, the cat! I was so excited when I had enough money to buy him as a pet. Right now though, I wish I'd thought to check my character's clothes and gear before logging in.

First thing first, this cat has got to go, he's massive! I shoo him away with my fingers, brushing his side to get him to leap off my shoulder.

"Fsst, get! That's a bad kitty!"

He jumps down and looks back at me balefully. Then he sits and starts grooming himself in a way that says "This is what I think of you, buddy."

My view of the pitch-black ceiling is blocked from sight as a person steps in front of me. I glance up, but I already know who it is.

"Welcome back, sleeping beauty," Kat says.

She is standing above me, leaning over. Her hair is falling into her face, and she's got her nose all scrunched up as she stares at me.

Either she's trying to figure out if I'm okay, or she's trying to find a kind way to tell me I smell bad.

I'm giving them equal odds.

"What? What are you looking at?" Yes, I'm being surly.

I mean I'm not hurt or anything, but Jumping is somewhat disorienting, and I need a minute to recover.

She's not going to give me a minute though, I can already tell. "I've just never seen anyone Jump into the game like you do, it's kind of odd."

"What did it look like?" In my head, it's super cool, like I materialize in, one pixel at a time, something you'd see in Star Trek.

The way she put emphasis on the word "odd" makes me think that's not what happened.

"Uh, well, you just sort of popped in about a foot from the ground, then fell on your butt. It actually kind of look like it might have hurt."

She reaches out and puts her hand on the back of my head, probing with her fingers.

None too gently, I might add.

"What are you doing?!" I jerk away from her, trying to stand up.

My foot starts to throb, so I sit back down, wincing.

"Geez, I just wanted to see if you had a bump. I mean it really looked like it hurt." She crosses her arms over her chest and seems to decide that she doesn't care if I'm hurt or not.

"Alright, Jed. I'm going to tell you what's going on." She places her hands on her hips. "If you're in, we have to act fast, and if you're out, well, we still have to act fast."

"Great. Tell me everything." Answers! I am going to get answers! "Start by telling me what a Jumper is."

"It's tough to explain." Sitting down on the dirt floor, she assumes a cross-legged position, like she's settling in to tell a long story.

"The easiest way for me to do it is to say that a Jumper is just a regular person, with a little extra coding."

"Coding"?" Are we talking DNA or something else?

"Sort of." She seems to understand where my thought process has gone. "You could say that we're a little more connected with cyberspace than the average kid. And this extra connection lets us do things that most kids can't do."

"Like walk into video games?"

"Not all video games, no." She shakes her head, her hair brushing her face. "This game is special. You wouldn't be able to Jump anywhere else."

"How do you know?" I mean how can she really be sure about that?

"You're just going to have to trust me when I say that this game is not what you think it is. The designers had much more in mind than a bit of mindless entertainment when they developed it.....when they developed you."

She looks at me, expectantly.

"You're saying someone programmed me?" I can't make this fit in my brain. "I'm a robot?"

"No, Jed," she puts her head in her hands, looking very tired all of the sudden. "You're a person, everything about you is human, you just have a little extra in there," she gestures in my direction.

"How did I get the "extra" in here?" I mimic her gesture.

"They put it there, and I wish this were relevant to the conversation because I know it feels relevant to you, but it's not. You're just going to have to understand that the "how" of it doesn't matter right now."

She pauses before continuing. "It will matter, and we'll deal with it, but for now, you've got to start here." She points to the ground at her feet in an emphatic gesture. "You've got to learn what you're capable of."

She stands up and walks over to me, then kneels down beside me and gestures around the cave. "I need your help, we need your help. But you're no good to anyone unless you let us help you figure out what you do here."

"We're not all the same, Jed. I've never seen anyone Jump the same as you do. But if you can do what I think you can do..." She hesitates, looking at me like she's willing me to understand. "If you can do what I think you can do, it could mean we've actually got a chance."

I sit there in the dirt and darkness thinking about this whole messed up situation. My brain keeps going back to the fact that Thomas is in this. He must trust her, or at least believe enough in what she's trying to do that he'd risk bringing me into it.

"Okay," I say, coming to a decision, "I'll wait on the "how" of it all, but only because I feel like it's not something I can change anyway."

I adjust my legs in front of me, reaching down to remove the shoe from my injured ankle. Kat watches me without comment.

"Tell me why, though. Why am I here? What do I need to do?"

She smiles at me, relief evident on her face.

"We're the First." She gestures between her and I. "We're the Beta kids. We're incomplete, which is why they want us back."

She shakes her head in a jerky, rapid motion. "You don't want to go back, Jed, believe me."

I'm trying to process all this. "Go back? Go back where? I've never been there."

"You have, Jed." She looks at me a little sadly, "You have, you just don't remember."

She takes the shoe I'm holding in my hand, setting it on the floor.

"It's okay though, I don't need you to remember." The look on her face says she wishes she didn't remember.

"I just need you to help me stop them from raising a generation of zombie kids."

"Them, who?"

"The Company." They way she says it, while staring at me intently, I get the impression she wants to see if I recognize the name.

I don't, I'm totally lost. "Which company?"

"That's their name, Jed."

Walking over to the fire, she kicks sand and dirt into it, watching the flames start to flicker and die.

"They don't talk about it more specifically, fancying themselves the world's biggest secret society or something." She says that part with a sneer. "They believe they're going to change the world, create a perfect place for everyone. A world where no one wants anything more than they have, and no one needs anything more than they're given. You'll have a place, they'll decide what that place is, and you will never have any desire to do more or less."

That sounds awful! Is this even possible?

"How would they even accomplish such a thing? They'd be taking away people's free will!"

"Yes," she looks at me like I'm finally getting something right, "they will take away your free will, and you won't.even.care."

"They've been working on this for years," she continues. "They're trying to put messages into products, commercials, games, etc. Messages that will affect how a person feels about that item. Beyond just liking it, to NEEDING it or DESPISING it."

I nod, indicating she should keep going.

"They've gotten so close to the makeup of the human brain with their programming. They've realized they can not only force a person to feel a certain way about a product, but if they start in the right place, they can bring up a whole generation of kids who are already attuned."

She walks over to the wall, grabbing a torch from a metal holder. Turning around, she goes back to the fire, kicking more dirt on it to snuff it out entirely.

"Wait," I stop her. "You mean they can make me do something I wouldn't normally do, only it'll be my idea?"

"Yes." she says. "Maybe you decide to drink a certain soda that you didn't used to like. Maybe you watch a TV show that never really appealed to you before. Maybe you play a game that you would never normally play. It's small things right now, but as you get older..... " she trails off, leaving me to fill in the blanks.

I shiver, hugging myself, and not just because of the cold in the cave.

The idea of my life not being my own, all my dreams....what if I woke up one day and they were gone? I wouldn't even know, would I? What if it's already happening to me? "Why am I here, then? Why this game? I don't understand."

"Right now, they don't have a good way to affect the entire population. They're working on it though, make no mistake about that." She pauses, considering her next words. "They have figured out a way to affect some people, though." She spreads her arms wide, indicating the world around us.

"Roblox....." I breathe, understanding dawning.

"Yes, Roblox." She nods.

"They've put something into the games, making them addictive for even the most casual player. We call it a beacon, but you can call it whatever you want." She begins to pace, the torch in her hand casting sinister shadows in what I used to think was a pretty cool place.

"It affects the coding of the game, placing the messages wherever they want them to be.

Players see the messages the first time they play, and...mission accomplished, they'll be coming back."

"And the more they come back, the more messages they see?" I phrase it as a question, even though I think I know the answer.

"Yes, again. As long as the beacon remains in this game, kids all over the world will keep coming back, even if they hate it. The beacon makes it the PERFECT game for you, no matter who you are, you'll love it."

I imagine myself wanting to play the "Beauty Shop" world for hours on end, and shudder.

"Why use Roblox for this? I mean, aren't there more insidious things they could be doing with this technology?"

"Yes, absolutely. They're in the infancy phase right now. They needed a place to test it that gave them a huge population, and also the right type of brain. It's no good to try it out on a brain that's not open to suggestion." She shrugs. "What better place than an online game? What better place than where kids spend hours at a time immersing themselves in a fantasy?"

"So you're saying they started here because our brains are easier to manipulate?" That realization feels....bad.

"That's exactly what I'm saying." Kat nods. "You believe it could happen, and therefore, it can happen. If they start now, we will be the generation that brings this technology to the future. Once they're in, they're hard to get out, so we'll grow into adulthood accepting this as the new normal."

"Um, yeah, when you put it that way...." I groan "So how do we stop them?"

"That's actually the easy part," she replies. "Remove the beacon, remove the link, the game goes back to normal. That's what Thomas has been helping us with."

Huh, that's a lot less dramatic than I thought it would be. Why do I feel like it won't actually turn out that way?

"So you want me to remove the beacon from this game?"

"You're such a good student." She pats me on the head. "Let's get going!"

"Whee," I think to myself. "I can't wait."

CHAPTER 10

DRINK THIS
THEN GO WRECK STUFF

"Find the beacon, smash it to pieces, go back home? Right?"

"Almost," Kat says. "We actually need to get the beacon, get to the carrier, get to the portal, and take the beacon through the portal."

"That sounds a lot more complicated, you just added like 15 steps."

"No, I didn't add any steps, you just left them out."

Semantics.

"Don't worry," she assures me, patting my arm. "Jake will be manning the copter, he knows when and where to pick you up. The portal is on the carrier, so you're going there anyway. We'll just keep the beacon with you, and you'll bring it home. Done!"

Is Jake coming? That actually makes me happy. I like him!

But.....she really makes it sound so easy when it's probably not going to be.

I'm thinking she might be an optimist.....or she just doesn't feel like dealing with my nerves anymore.

"Alright, well let's go then," I try to stand up again.

I keep forgetting about my stupid foot!

Nevermind, I'll walk when there's just no other way.

"Where's the beacon?"

"It's in the ocean, beneath the carrier." She starts walking toward one of the walls, getting further and further from me.

"What?! It's where?!" No one said anything about an ocean.

"How am I supposed to get down there? I know I can't bring stuff into Roblox with me, but I can definitely bring things out. This busted up ankle came home last time, and it's still here." I gesture to my foot. How can she not have noticed?

"I can hardly walk, let alone run, let alone swim."

"Not to worry, Jed. I've got you covered."

Huh, I guess she did notice.

She holds up her right hand and makes a "mouse click" motion into the air with her fingers.

Up pops MY game inventory! It hovers in the air, right in the middle of the cave.

I stare in awe as dust motes float through the picture.

"Oh my gosh! That is so cool! How did you do that?!"

"Tricks of the trade, my friend." She smirks, looking extremely pleased with herself, and with my reaction.

She scans my inventory for a second, then reaches up and plucks the blue bottle out of the bag slot. She holds it in her hand and walks back over to me, extending her arm, indicating that I should take it.

"What is it?" I eye it skeptically.

"Healing potion!" She says this in the same manner a magician would say "Ta-Da!"

"So I can't bring anything into the game, but I can use in-game items, and they work?"

That's pretty cool, at least.

"Sometimes, on some things anyway. If you drink this though, your ankle will be as good as new!"

She looks so triumphant right now that I can't help but smile at her.

I uncork the bottle, give it a sniff (it smells like the inside of a wet shoe, again), hold my nose, and drink it down.

It tastes awful, like I just took a swig of spoiled milk.

"Ughhhh! That is vile! You should have warned me!"

"If I warned you, you wouldn't have drank it."

She's right.

My ankle starts to feels uncomfortably tight, then gets a tingling sensation. It's like I fell asleep on it, then tried to stand up.

The pins and needles feeling happens, and I hop around going "Oww, oww, oww, ahh, ahh, ahh," for a few seconds, until it settles down.

I stand up and take a couple of ginger steps, just to see how it feels. It's entirely normal, no pain at all. "Awesome! That is completely cool!"

"Ready?" She asks.

"It's a rhetorical question, isn't it?"

"Yes, yes it is."

I put my sock and shoe back on, stand up, and follow her to the wall of the cave.

We're off.

CHAPTER 11

STEP 1: DON'T LET ZOMBIES BITE YOUR FACE

I'm standing there wondering how we're getting out of the cave when Kat brushes past me and walks over to a wall, pushing aside a clump of branches.

There's the opening I couldn't see earlier.

I really am Captain Observant.

We walk out of the cave, practically onto the beach where Jake will pick us up in the helicopter.

I've got my "in-game" gun, she's got some kind of wicked looking spiked mace, and it doesn't take long for the zombies to spot us.

I'm not super concerned, we're so close to the pickup point that we should be able to hop right into Jake's copter as soon as he lands.

I keep forgetting the most essential rule of Jumping though. Understandable since this is only my second time.

Remember that movie "Wreck-It Ralph"? The part where they're in between the video games? There's this voice over the loudspeakers saying "If you die outside your game, you won't come back. It's game over, forever."

It takes me only a few seconds to go from "I'm gonna wreck it!" to "No cuts, No buts, No coconuts." as I knock other players out of the way trying to get to the base.

I can hear the whir of the chopper in the distance. I am not missing out on my ride!

This is where "JackPlaysStuff" and I will be different. No offense, bro, but I'm gonna be one and done!

Kat's yelling for me to slow down, so I do (a little) and let her catch up.

What can I say, I'm 10, chivalry isn't really a thing for me yet, and she's older.

I'm the one who needs protecting here.

We round the bend, and there's the base looming before us. We just have to run twenty or so steps up in a semicircle to the top. Once we do, we're there, standing between the turrets.

I crane my neck to stare at the helicopter easing down PAINFULLY SLOWLY in front of us.

After a forever amount of minutes pass, Jake finally touches down.

I run the rest of the way to the helicopter, grab the nylon loop hanging from the edge, and hop in.

There are no doors, so I wrap the loop around my wrist and hang on tight. Jake looks back at me and nods his head. I give him a thumbs up, and he starts the ascent.

The copter takes off, and I look out the open bay doors. I'm staring down at the place where I was just standing, where Kat is now standing, alone!

"Jake!" I yell up at him. "You left Kat! We have to go back and get her!"

"Sorry, Jed!" Jake yells back, shrugging his shoulders. "Glitch of the game, blame the makers, but this bird only holds two people, and today that's you and me!"

Kat's form grows smaller in the distance. I see her hurrying away from a mob of zombies surrounding the base. I hope she's going to the cave.

Jake's voice jerks me out of my stupor. "Don't worry about her, Jed! She's the oldest of us! She knows how to take care of herself!"

I don't respond, so he yells again. "Are you with me!? We've still got a job to do, so head in the game!"

I nod. "I know! I've got to get the beacon, where is it?!"

He jerks his head in front of us, off to the left, where an enormous carrier covered in helicopters lies in wait.

"It's down there!" He says. "See the anchor chain?! Follow it down! The beacon is at the bottom!"

I nod again, leaving my motion to serve as an answer.

It's so loud, and I'm mightily sick of screaming over the noise of these rotors.

I look toward the front of the carrier at the massive metal chain hanging in the water. The links are enormous, they must be a solid 5 feet across, and at least twice that high.

How am I going to get down there? More importantly, how am I going to get back UP once I'm done?

"Jake! How am I going to get down there!? And how am I going to get back up once I'm done!?"

Hey, it was important, I had to ask more than just myself.

"There's a metal wire attached to a buoy in the water! Swim to the buoy and grab the handle that's attached to the wire! It'll pull you down to the beacon!"

He pauses like he remembered something important.

"There's a small air tank attached the buoy as well, it's only good for 5 minutes or so! Once you get the beacon, use the handle to get back to the surface, and I'll drop a rope down for you!"

This sounds so incredibly complicated, what could possibly go wrong?

I'm just about to voice this..... utterly rational thought to Jake when he yells again.

"There's the buoy, see you when you get back!"

Then he yanks the stick, tips the helicopter to the left, and unceremoniously dumps me into the ocean.

CHAPTER 12

ZIP LINES ARE SUPPOSED TO BE FUN!

I can still hear the helicopter above me, but I can't see anything. The saltwater is stinging my eyes.

"This is a video game!" I yell toward the helicopter. "Why can't the saltwater not sting!?"

I don't get an answer.

Swimming to the buoy doesn't take long. It's actually quite large, dipping and bobbing in the waves.

It's something like the size of a big beach ball, and just as colorful.

There are alternating red and yellow stripes that start full at the top and taper toward the bottom, ending in a hard, black rubber base.

There's a wire attached to the base, and a carabiner locked around the wire. The wire is holding the buoy to what I assume must be whatever is anchoring it to the ocean floor.

The air tank is attached to that carabiner, so I unclip it, gripping it tightly. It's quite small, but I suppose it would have to be.

I'm going to need to hang on to both the handle and the tank as I'm propelled toward the bottom of the sea.

Someone has also thoughtfully provided me with a pair of goggles. They are attached to the carabiner as well, so I slip them off, looping them around my wrist as I kick my feet, keeping my head above water.

I have to push them up to my elbow because they keep trying to float away in the swells.

Alright, no time like the present! I pull the goggles down my arm, bring them up to my head, and snap them over my face, wincing as the rubber pulls at the short hairs on the back of my head.

I wrap one hand around the black plastic handle of the zip line and grab the air tank in the other.

I can't really tell you which one I'm holding on to more tightly.

If I had kids, I'd say it would be like choosing my favorite child.

Who am I kidding? It's the air tank, I'm holding on to the air tank tighter.

I'm apparently going to be a terrible father.

I place the air tank over my mouth, holding it tightly to my face to create a seal. Then I push a button on the handle of the zip line, and it starts towing me rapidly down into the depths.

My ears pop, I don't bother clearing them since I don't think this is going to be a short trip.

I can see little more than brown, murky sediment. Even with the goggles on I only know I've hit bottom when I actually....hit bottom.

It's a soft sort of thud though, definitely better than jumping off a 10-foot prison wall.

I stand still for a few precious moments, holding the air tank to my face. I'm waiting for the sediment to settle back on the ocean floor so I can see again.

Gradually, a soft white glow starts to come from the exact place where the anchor and ocean floor meet.

Letting go of the zip line, I swim toward that point. My eardrums are painful by now, but I don't dare remove the air tank to try and fix them. Instead I focus on the glowing white light, the faster I get it, the faster I can get back to the surface.

When I reach it, I see that the beacon is quite small, nothing like I thought it would be. I'm not sure what I thought it would be, maybe a cube of some sort, a diamond that stands on end? Whatever it looked like in my head, it was way more impressive than this.

It does glow, but that's about all I can say for it.

If I had to describe it in a way everyone would understand, I'd say it looks sort of like a trophy. The kind you'd get for "participation" on a little league baseball team.

It's tarnished, made of gold plastic, and the marble-esque base is chipped. The nameplate appears to be some sort of metal. I can tell because it's rusting.

The place where a name would go is both blank and hanging off the edge because only one of the rivets is still intact.

It's like someone walked to the bow of the ship and chunked a trophy off of it. The thought makes me smile.

"Go, Team!" I'd make a great cheerleader.

I swim back to the zipline much more slowly. One hand holds the air tank to my face, the other grips the beacon, so I have to move using only my feet.

It's not easy.

When I get there, I have to make a decision. I can't hold the air tank, the beacon, and the zip line.

Something has to go.

I take a last big gulp of oxygen, then let the tank drop, watching as it slips lazily to the ocean floor.

Goodbye favorite child!

I grip the zip line handle tightly, press the button, and feel a wave of nausea as my body is jerked upward. My ears don't clear, so I hold my nose and pop them the moment my head pops out of the waves.

Then, while treading water with one hand, I turn in circles, looking around.

I spot Jake's copter in the sky, and below it, a basket dangles from a rope, mostly submerged in the water.

I swim over and realize that it's not a full-sized body basket, more like a woven hammock.

The message is clear, "Put your butt here." So I do.

Jake lifts the chopper, and in no time flat, I'm being dropped off on the black tarmac airstrip of the carrier.

CHAPTER 13

SHHHH! OMG SHOOSH!!!!

I stand there, a bit dumbly, for a minute, getting my bearings. Helicopters are landing all over the place. I see players running around, and new helicopters taking off.

I don't see Jake or his copter anywhere.

Did he fly off after he left me? Is he coming back? Do I stand here and wait?

I'm wet and cold, my clothes are soaked again, and my teeth are chattering, despite the relative warmth of the island air.

A rush of wind over my head makes my decision for me, at the very least, I am getting away from this airstrip.

You know that scene in "Indiana Jones" where the guy gets chopped up in an airplane propeller? I read somewhere that it actually happened. Like the guy died while he was filming that scene.

If it could happen to him, a paid stuntman....well heck, I haven't got a chance.

There's a large, central area on the carrier, it must be the place the captain stands when he needs to steer the ship. It sticks up about 30 feet from the airstrip level, and the very top of it is nothing but windows all the way around. It almost looks like the central tower at an airport, with spinning sonar and radar arms fixed to the roof.

I can't really see the point of it since the ship doesn't move in this game, but I guess they want to keep it looking authentic.

Below that though, there's a door. It's average sized, metal, and built into the framework of the ship. If I had to guess, I'd bet that's my entrance into the hallway that will get me to the Captain's Quarters, and OUT of this game.

Getting to the door is simple, the commotion out here makes it easy to blend in and disappear. Once I get inside though, I look around and realize there are no other players in here with me. It's entirely empty, and that means it'll be all that much easier to get caught if someone (Dirk) is tracking me.

I'm actually surprised I haven't seen him yet. I hope my luck holds out.

Directly inside the door, there's only one way to go. A metal staircase leads down to the interior of the ship. I guess the part up top is just for show, because I can't see any way to get up there.

I follow the stairs down, taking care to step lightly. There's a rail attached to the wall (hull? I have no idea what it's called), and I hold on to it with one hand, still grasping the beacon in the other.

I reach the bottom of the steps, coming to a stop in a long hallway. I mean it's REALLY long, it must run the entire length of the carrier. There are doors spaced every 10 feet or so on both the right and left side.

At the very end, way down there, I can make out an ornate wooden door. It's decorated with gold fixtures and an old-time ship's wheel.

That must be the Captain's Quarters.

I hear a noise behind me, so I hustle forward and duck into the first door I come to. Drops of water splatter behind me, no doubt making a wonderful trail for anyone to follow, if they want to.

The room is empty, there's not even a way to close the door, so I move to one side and push my back against the wall, listening.

Nothing happens. No one comes. Silence reigns.

I'm about to leave the room when I feel something brush against my leg.

I jump away, freaked out!

Turning quickly, I see what bumped into me. It's that cat, the one I pushed off my shoulder!

Never in my life have I more regretted picking that option when I dressed my character.

The cat starts to climb my pant leg, digging its sharp little claws into the fabric, and "Ouch!" skin. Apparently, its goal is to once again sit on my shoulder.

"No, no, bad cat, bad!" I whisper at it, but really harshly so it knows I mean business.

I'm not a cat fan, what can I say?

If Roblox had a dog that would sit on your shoulder, I'd be all about it, but instead, I settled for what I could get.

Gently removing the cat's claws from my skin, I place it on the ground. Then I peek out of the room, see that coast is clear, and continue down the hallway.

The cat is following me, I can hear the slight "tap, tap, tap" of his claws on the metal floor. Every few feet, he winds himself around my legs and says "Meow!"

"Shhhh, oh my gosh, shhh!" I have no idea what to do with this cat, so I pick him up, untuck my shirt, stuff him under, and re-tuck it.

I feel like a kangaroo, or maybe a pregnant woman.

Okay no, not that, that's a terrible comparison.

I feel like an idiot, there we go!

I'm walking down the hallway, holding a busted up baseball trophy. I've got a squirming, furry mass hanging over the waistband of my jeans, and I'm trying to be stealthy.

I put my free hand over the cat-mound to try and keep him still.

There's no one coming down the hall, the coast appears to be clear. I power walk the last few yards to the wooden door, briefly remove my hand from the shirt cat, and try the handle.

It's unlocked!

"Yes!" Again, I whisper, but I follow it up with a fist pump!

I push open the door, and peek my head around the edge.

This room, like all of the others, is also empty. There's only one thing in it, the jello/fog portal standing proudly in the center of the space.

It's my way home.

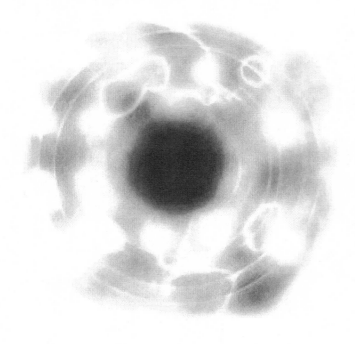

CHAPTER 14

COOL CATS, BAD DOGS, AND "THAT GUY KNOWS JUDO?"

I walk right up to the portal, thinking this is going to be easy, that I'm in the clear. Only, when I get to it and reach out my hand, my fingers pass right through, like it's not there. I can see the portal, but I can't touch it, and I cannot see my room on the other side.

Do I need to activate it?

There's gotta be something around here that will turn it on.

I look around once again, but it's empty, there's NOTHING here!

"What's the matter, Jed? Are you....stuck?"

I whirl around to face the person who came into the room behind me.

"Seriously, I heard the cat, but I don't hear you?" It comes out more sarcastic than scared, and for that I am grateful.

Dirk faces me, smiling his evil little smile.

I want to dunk his head in a toilet bowl.

"Dude, what is your problem? Why are you helping these people?"

"Why!? How about a little recognition?!" He screams it, going from zero to sixty in no time flat.

"Do you know what it's like to be the school outcast? The one no one hangs with at lunch, the guy people pick last for dodgeball?"

He's ranting, pacing back and forth, arms waving wildly as he lists off all the injustices done to him.

"Do you have any idea how many times my shoes have been stolen and thrown on to overhead telephone wires? Do you know how many wedgies I've been given? It's my turn to win!"

All I can think is that I can't believe he's in cahoots with "The Company" over such trivial things. Dodgeball? Wedgies?

Is he insane?

He's really getting worked up though, so I change tactics.

"I get it, Dirk, but this is your chance to do something good, you can help me get out of here. Help me destroy the beacon, give these gamers back their free will."

"I don't WANT them to have free will!" he screams. His face is turning all red, and I'm pretty sure he just got some spit on me.

I take my hand off the "cat bundle" and wipe at my face with the back of my hand.

Gross.

The movement dislodges my tucked in shirt, and the cat sticks his face out.

As soon as he sees Dirk, he goes bananas. Hissing, spitting, clawing!

I jump back and pull my shirt up the rest of the way so the cat can get away from me. He's like a black blur, straight to Dirk. Up Dirk's pants, onto his shirt, and right up in his face.

Dirk is batting at him like mad, trying to get away, but this cat is angry!

This cat is also way more awesome than I thought.

I hear footsteps pounding down the hallway. "Please don't let it be more Dirk cronies," I think to myself.

Jake comes running in the door, and I let out a relieved sigh.

"Jed, open your inventory!" He runs to Dirk and starts to wrestle him to the ground.

It's comical, Jake, Dirk, the black cat, all in a jumble of loud noises and hissing.

It takes me a second to realize what he's talking about. My inventory? OH! Like Kat did in the cave!

I raise my right hand, pretend I'm holding on to a mouse, and *click*.

Up pops my inventory!

"What do I do now?!"

"The Redstone Block! Just click it!"

I hover my cursor over the block, then left click to use it. The timer bar pops up at the bottom of the screen again, counting down as the bar fills with white light.

I look up at the portal, my room starts to come into view.

There's my bed, the Redstone Block innocently perched on my pillow, and Ty.

My dog is standing on my bed, staring intently at the portal that must be appearing in front of him.

The timer finishes, the jello/fog becomes tangible, and I grab the beacon even harder. The last thing I want is to lose it before I walk through.

At that moment, the cat lets out an angry "Mrowr!", and I can see what's going to happen even before it does.

Ty's ears perk up, his whole body goes taut, and that hump of fur between his shoulder blades stands straight up on end.

"Ty, no! Stay!" I try to stop him, but it's too late.

Ty sees the cat, and the cat sees Ty.

The cat jumps off of Dirk and darts out the door, back into the hallway.

Ty jumps into the portal, and all the sudden, he's right there with me, in the Captain's Quarters. I lunge for his collar, but he's gone, through the door, down the hall, and out of sight.

"Ty!" I run toward the door, but Jake jumps in front of me.

"No! You have to go! There's no time!"

"I am not leaving my dog! Get out of my way!"

I shove him, hard!

He backs up a few steps, looking at me, assessing.

Dirk runs out of the room, and I can see that Jake is torn between getting me through the portal, and going after him.

He holds up both of his hands in a "calm down" sort of gesture, seeming to come to a decision.

"It's okay, it's okay, I get it. You can stay, go find your dog, I'll tell Kat to help you. Just give me the beacon and I'll go back through for you."

I don't even think twice, I reach my hand out to him, ready to give him the beacon.

It was too easy.

Jake grabs my wrist in a classic Judo hold, falls to the ground, and smoothly kicks me over his shoulder, into the portal.

I land in a heap on my floor.

My last sight is of Jake clicking something in the air, and the portal is gone.

COME SEE TY PLAY ROBLOX!

I video myself playing these games for the first time, so come check it out!

Click Here for Rescue Mission Zombie Assault, or go to www.TyTheHunter.com and click
VIDEOS
Don't forget to SUBSCRIBE!

Please leave a review,
they're so important.

The more reviews you leave,
the more books I write.

Ty

P.S. - Don't forget to ask your parents to download your free short story at

NEXT IN THE SERIES

The World Keepers - Book 3

Other Books By Ty The Hunter

The Guild Crafters Series
Ages 9 +

The Guild Crafers Block Books Series
Ages 4 +

35450109R00090

Made in the USA
San Bernardino, CA
10 May 2019